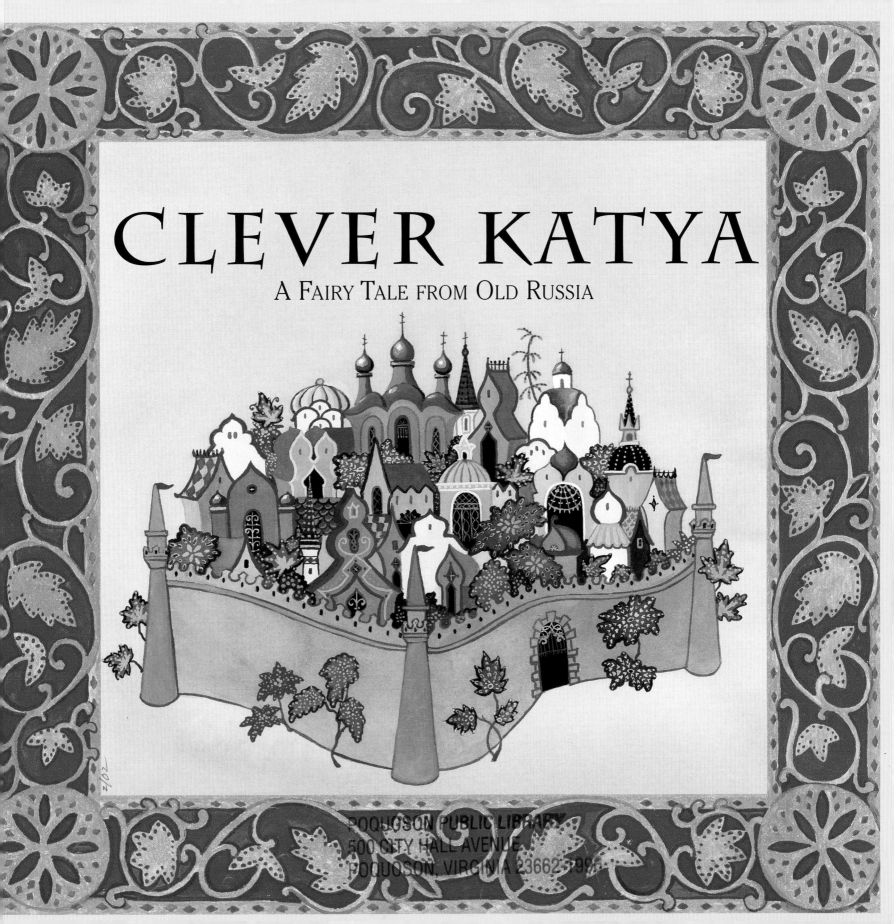

CLEVER KATYA

A Fairy Tale from Old Russia

For Olivia Charlotte, a very clever little girl – *M.H.*
For Grandma, with much love – *M.C.*

Barefoot Books
41 Schermerhorn Street, Suite 145
Brooklyn, New York
NY 11201-4845

Library of Congress Cataloging-in-Publication Data available on request

ISBN 1 901223 64 7

Graphic design by Design/Section, Frome
Color reproduction by Grafiscan, Verona
Printed and bound in Singapore by Tien Wah Press Pte Ltd

1 3 5 7 9 8 6 4 2

CLEVER KATYA

A FAIRY TALE FROM OLD RUSSIA

Retold by MARY HOFFMAN   Illustrated by MARIE CAMERON

BAREFOOT BOOKS

nce upon a time, in a village in Russia, there were two brothers. One was rich and the other poor, but they both kept horses. That was how the villagers earned their living, by breeding horses.

The older brother, Dmitri, was so good at it and had grown so rich that he gave his poor brother Ivan one of his mares. And because Ivan had no pasture, Dmitri let the mare graze with his own horses.

One day the two brothers set out to market. Dmitri was riding a fine white stallion and Ivan was carried by the little brown mare his brother had given him.

As night fell, they stopped by an empty hut and tethered their horses outside. Inside was a pile of hay where they lay down to sleep as best they could.

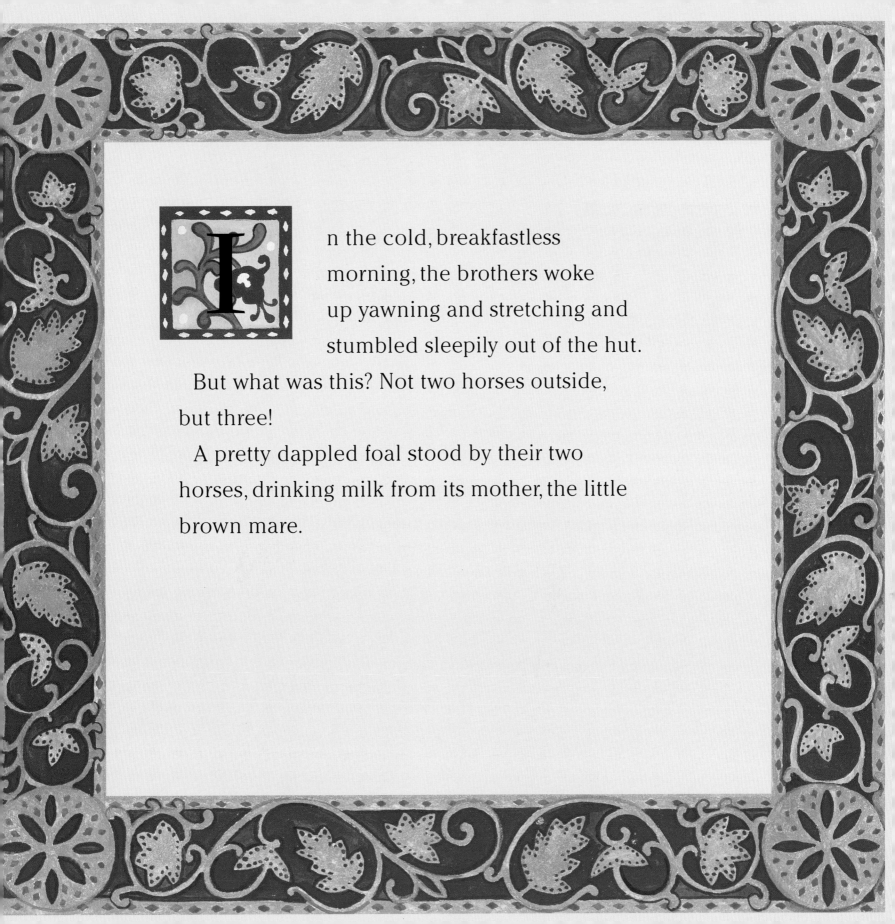

I n the cold, breakfastless morning, the brothers woke up yawning and stretching and stumbled sleepily out of the hut.

But what was this? Not two horses outside, but three!

A pretty dappled foal stood by their two horses, drinking milk from its mother, the little brown mare.

"The foal's mine!" cried Dmitri, who was as greedy as he was rich. Ivan didn't like to argue but this didn't seem fair to him.

"Surely, since my mare gave birth to the foal, it must be mine?" he said.

"Nonsense!" snapped Dmitri. "My stallion is clearly the father. And besides, I gave you the mare in the first place. I said nothing about giving you a foal too!"

T he two brothers glared at one another, all thought of their work at the market forgotten.

"We'll settle this once and for all," said Dmitri. "We'll put the matter before the judges in town."

So they got on their horses and rode slowly into town, the wobbly little foal trotting along behind them.

n the market square, the young Tsar had taken the place of the usual judges. It was a special day when, once a year, the Tsar amused himself by hearing the local people's cases. He was an intelligent man with a quirky sense of humor.

When the two brothers came before him, his mouth began to twitch. This was going to be an especially amusing case. The Tsar knew perfectly well that Dmitri had no claim on the foal but he decided to have a bit of fun at the brothers' expense while indulging his fondness for riddles at the same time.

"I can't decide between you," he said, "but I shall award the foal to whichever of you can solve these four riddles. What is the fastest thing in the world, what is the fattest, what is the softest and what the most precious? Come to my palace in a week's time with your answers."

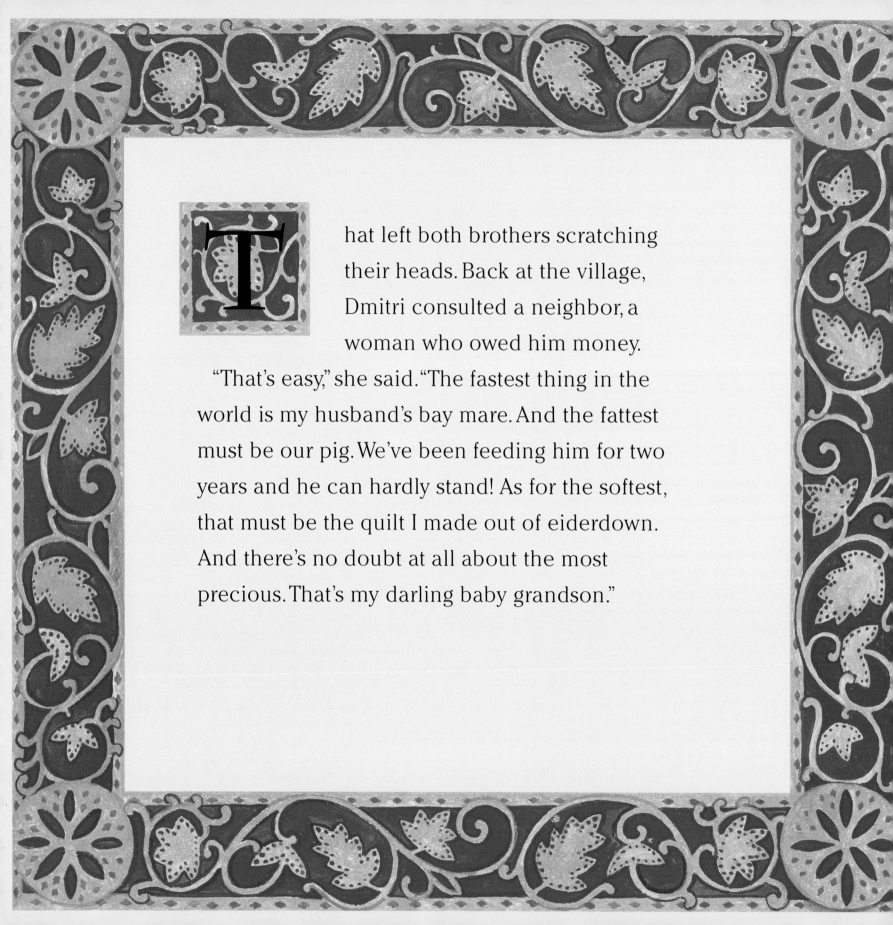

That left both brothers scratching their heads. Back at the village, Dmitri consulted a neighbor, a woman who owed him money.

"That's easy," she said. "The fastest thing in the world is my husband's bay mare. And the fattest must be our pig. We've been feeding him for two years and he can hardly stand! As for the softest, that must be the quilt I made out of eiderdown. And there's no doubt at all about the most precious. That's my darling baby grandson."

Ivan meanwhile had gone home to his small daughter, Katya, who was only seven. She was delighted when she saw the pretty little foal.

"Aye, but we won't be able to keep it unless I can answer the Tsar's riddles," said Ivan and told her the whole story.

Now Katya was a very thoughtful child, who had spent a lot of time on her own since her mother died.

"Don't worry, Father," she said. "I'll give you the answers. The fastest thing is the wind that rushes over the Steppes. The fattest is the earth, which feeds everyone and everything on it. The softest is a child's caress – feel that, Father. It is, isn't it? And the most precious is honesty."

hen the two brothers turned up at the palace, the Tsar could scarcely hide his laughter at Dmitri's answers, particularly when he said the most precious thing in the world was his neighbor's grandson.

But he grew thoughtful when Ivan gave his answers, especially the one about honesty. He knew that he himself hadn't been quite honest with the brothers.

"Who told you these answers?" he asked.

"My little daughter, Katya, Your Majesty," replied Ivan.

"A wise child indeed. Very well, you shall have the foal and a hundred silver ducats too, but on one condition. In a week's time, you must bring Katya to my palace."

Ivan was very relieved and began to bow in thanks.

"Just a minute!" said the Tsar sternly. "She must be neither on horseback nor on foot, neither naked nor dressed and neither bringing a present nor empty-handed.

I f she can appear like this, the foal and the money are yours. If not, I shall have your head removed."

Back home, Ivan was now in the deepest despair and would have given up the foal at once. For what use would a foal be to Katya if her father had his head cut off?

Katya guessed that the Tsar was only bluffing but she was too practical to take any chances.

"Get me a hare and a partridge, Father," she said, "but make sure they're both alive. Then bring me your fishing-net."

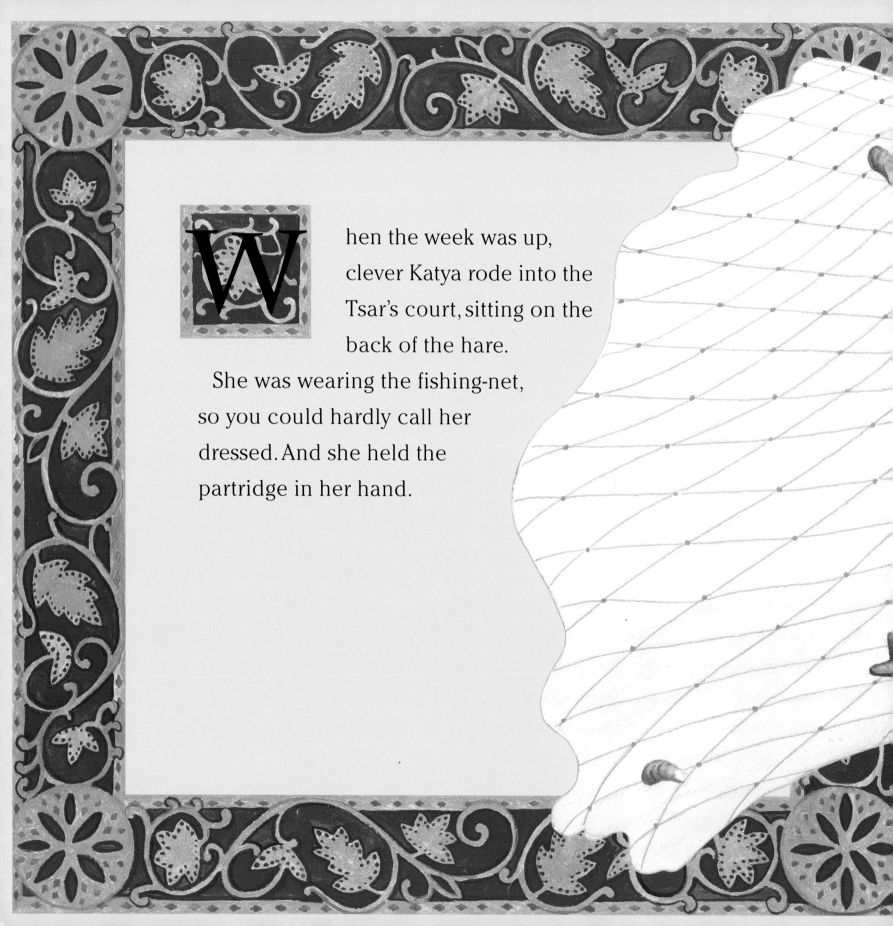

hen the week was up, clever Katya rode into the Tsar's court, sitting on the back of the hare.

She was wearing the fishing-net, so you could hardly call her dressed. And she held the partridge in her hand.

T he Tsar knew he had met his match, but he tried to keep up his pretence.

"Is that a present for me?" he asked, pointing at the bird.

"Take it," said Katya simply, releasing the partridge, which immediately flew up to the rafters.

The Tsar was intrigued by this clever peasant-child. "What do you and your father live on?" he asked.

"Why," said Katya, "on the hares like these that father catches in the rivers and the fish I trap in the trees with this net I'm wearing."

"But that's absurd!" said the Tsar, in spite of himself. "How can you find hares in the river and fish in the trees?"

"As easily as you'll find a stallion giving birth to a foal, Your Majesty," replied Katya modestly.

The whole court held its breath. And then the Tsar burst into gales of laughter.

"Only in my kingdom could such a clever little girl be found!" he declared. After that everyone joined in the laughter.

So everything ended happily for Ivan, who was now just as rich as Dmitri.

As for Katya, she became a great favorite of the Tsar's and when she was grown up, she married him and became Tsarina of all Russia, because she was the only woman in the kingdom clever enough for him.

AUTHOR'S NOTE

I first came across this story when I was researching a completely different book. I do a lot of re-tellings of myths, legends, folk and fairy tales, and I was surfing the net for possible material. Using the latest technology to locate some of the oldest stories, many of which come originally from oral cultures, is a paradox which appeals to me. This is how I chanced upon *The Wise Little Girl*.

I don't know how I had managed to miss this tale, as it has just the sort of ingredients I like: the weak gets the better of the strong, the child of the adult, the female of the male – great stuff! Shortly afterwards, I bought *The Virago Book of Fairy Tales*, edited by another heroine, the late Angela Carter. The story of *The Wise Little Girl* was there too, and Carter says in a note that it is her favorite in the collection.

The version Carter uses is a little different from the one here, and is taken from Alexandr Afanasiev's *Russian Fairy Tales*. Afanasiev does not give anyone in the story a name and there is a middle round of seemingly impossible tasks which the little girl completes.

My Internet sources call the brothers Dmitri and Ivan, and introduce the beheading penalty. But I gave Katya her name myself, on the grounds that the most important person in the story should not be anonymous.

The task that is set by the Tsar uses common folktale motifs, found also in the writing of Saxo Grammaticus, *The Mabinogion* and in the Irish tale of Diarmuid and Grainne, where someone must go neither naked nor clothed, neither on horseback nor on foot. These complex conditions, which often also include "neither eating nor fasting," must be met as part of a ritual ceremony to bring about marriage in some cases, or death in others. So it seems quite appropriate that, having met his challenges, Katya should become the young Tsar's wife when she is old enough.

Mary Hoffman

Sources:
The Virago Book of Fairy Tales, ed. Angela Carter, Virago Books 1991
HYPERLINK www.ece.ucdavis.edu/~darsie/tales.html
HYPERLINK www.swarthmore.edu/~sjohnson/archive.htm